LOST IN THE JUNGLE OF DOOM

TRACEY TURNER

Crabtree Publishing Company
www.crabtreebooks.com
1-800-387-7650

616 Welland Ave.
St. Catharines, ON
L2M 5V6

PMB 59051, 350 Fifth Ave.
59th Floor,
New York, NY

Published by Crabtree Publishing Company in 2015.

Author: Tracey Turner

Illustrator: Nelson Evergreen

Project coordinator: Kelly Spence

Editor: Alex Van Tol, Kathy Middleton

Proofreader: Wendy Scavuzzo

Prepress technician: Ken Wright

Print and Production coordinator: Katherine Berti

WARNING!

The instructions in this book are for extreme survival situations only. Always proceed with caution, and ask an adult to supervise—or, if possible, seek expert help. If in doubt, consult a responsible adult.

First published 2014 by A & C Black, an imprint of Bloomsbury Publishing Plc.

Printed in Canada/102014/EF20140925

Library and Archives Canada Cataloguing in Publication

Turner, Tracey, author
Lost in the jungle of doom / Tracey Turner.

(Lost : can you survive?)
Includes index.
ISBN 978-0-7787-0727-1 (bound).--
ISBN 978-0-7787-0735-6 (pbk.)

1. Plot-your-own stories. I. Title.

PZ7.T883Los 2014 j823'.92
C2014-904013-X

Library of Congress Cataloging-in-Publication Data

Turner, Tracey.
Lost in the jungle of doom / by Tracey Turner ; illustration, Nelson Evergreen. -- American edition.
pages cm. -- (Lost: can you survive?)
Includes index.
ISBN 978-0-7787-0727-1 (reinforced library binding) -- ISBN 978-0-7787-0735-6 (pbk.)
1. Plot-your-own stories. [1. Rain forests--Fiction. 2. Survival--Fiction. 3. Amazon River Region--Fiction. 4. Plot-your-own stories.] I. Evergreen, Nelson, 1971- illustrator. II. Title.

PZ7.T8585Los 2014
[Fic]--dc23

2014022788

Contents

South America

Caracas
Port-of-Spain
VENEZUELA
Georgetown
Paramaribo
Cayenne
GUYANA
SURINAME
FRENCH GUIANA
ATLANTIC OCEAN
Bogota
COLOMBIA
Quito
ECUADOR
Amazon Rainforest
PERU
BRAZIL
Lima
Brasilia
La Paz
BOLIVIA
PARAGUAY
Asuncion
PACIFIC OCEAN
CHILE
URUGUAY
Santiago
Buenos Aires
Montevideo
ARGENTINA
SOUTH ATLANTIC OCEAN
Stanley
FALKLAND ISLANDS

Welcome to your adventure!

STOP! Read this first!

Welcome to an action-packed adventure in which you take the starring role!

You're about to enter the Amazon Rainforest, where danger lurks at every turn. Choose from different options on each page, according to your instincts, knowledge, and intelligence, and make your own path through the jungle to safety.

You decide:

- How to escape a ferocious jaguar;
- Which foods you can eat, and which could be poisonous;
- How to survive rivers teeming with piranha;

. . . and many more life-or-death dilemmas. Along the way, you'll discover the facts you need to help you survive.

It's time to test your survival skills—or die trying!

Your adventure starts on page 7.

A harsh squawk jolts you awake. You open your eyes. In the dim, greenish light, tree trunks stretch into the distance in all directions. A red-and-yellow parrot swoops up to the top of a tree far above you in the forest canopy.

You try to get up but something is holding you down. It's a seatbelt. You're sitting in what used to be your airplane seat.

The events that brought you here come flooding back to you in a sickening rush: the bumpy flight in a small plane, the crash as something hit one of the propellers, then the terrible silence after the engine sputtered and died and the plane began to plummet . . .

You don't remember anything else. You must have blacked out. But, by some miracle, you alone survived. You unfasten the seatbelt with shaking hands and check for wounds: apart from some painful bruises and a few scratches, you are fine. Another miracle.

You were flying from Bogota in Colombia to Rio de Janeiro in Brazil. You calculate that you must be somewhere in the middle of the Amazon Rainforest. You are completely lost and, apparently, alone.

You set off with nothing but the clothes on your back, your trusty Swiss Army knife, and a dented metal container you find in the wreck.

How will you survive?

Turn to page 8 to find information you need to help you survive.

The Amazon Rainforest is the largest rainforest in the world, stretching for more than 1.9 million square miles (five million sq km) across the top half of South America. More than 30 million people live in the Amazon, most living in towns and cities, but some in the rainforest itself. Hundreds of thousands of different plant and animal species live there, too. It's so vast and so hazardous that many people have walked into the Amazon Rainforest never to be seen again. If you're going to survive, you'll need to have your wits about you.

Perils of the Rainforest

The Amazon is home to several large and deadly predators, including black caimans, jaguars, cougars, anacondas (the world's largest snake), and electric eels. Small, but dangerous, creatures include poison dart frogs, piranhas, vampire bats, venomous snakes and spiders, and biting insects that can transmit life-threatening diseases such as malaria, yellow fever, and dengue fever. There are also the terrible dangers of poisonous plants, water-borne diseases, and flash floods, which are common in the Amazon.

Vicious Vegetation

There aren't many low-growing plants on the rainforest floor. Because of the dense tree canopy, there's not very much light to make them grow. You'll have to negotiate tree roots and trailing creepers, but at least you won't need to slash through thick undergrowth. There are lots of thorny plants, though. Some of them can irritate your skin as well as scratch you, so watch out. You also need to be careful of the leaf litter on the forest floor where slithering snakes can often be found lurking, ready to attack their prey.

Night Noises

The rainforest can be a noisy place, especially at night. There are hundreds of different types of frogs that make whistles, shrieks, and even knocking sounds. There are more than a hundred species of monkeys. The loudest are howler monkeys, that make an alarming screech that can be heard for miles! You'll get used to the noises of the jungle if you stay here for awhile but, in the short term, you're going to have to tell yourself not to worry about them too much.

Turn to page 10.

Jungle Survival Tips

- The right clothing is essential to protect you from thorny and poisonous plants, biting insects, spiders and other creepy-crawlies, and snakes. You need sturdy boots, and you should cover as much of your skin as possible. Luckily, you are wearing jeans, a hooded sweatshirt, and hiking boots, and have a thin waterproof jacket bundled up in a pocket along with your trusty Swiss Army knife.

- Bacteria breeds quickly in the jungle, so stay as clean as possible. Wash in running water, and remember to wash your clothes, too.

- Wash and dry out your feet and footwear, too, or you might get warm water immersion foot from walking in wet footwear. It can be extremely painful and, if left untreated, can become infected and lead to death.

- Always check the ground for snakes as you walk. Many are well camouflaged and some are deadly. Use a stick and swish it in front of you to uncover dangers and warn small creatures away.

- Wash any cuts and scratches with boiled water, if possible. They can easily become infected if you don't. Luckily you remember to search the plane wreck before setting off, and you find a slightly dented metal container that you can boil water in.

The light is failing. Soon it will be completely dark. You can't begin your journey in darkness, and you need to be safe from night-hunting predators, that will be able to see you far more easily than you can see them. You need shelter. You spot a cave not far away. Should you sleep there, or use some of your valuable energy to build your own shelter?

If you decide to sleep in the cave, go to page 12.

If you decide to build your own shelter, go to page 14.

You make your way toward the cave in the twilight, stepping over gnarled tree roots and pushing past dangling creepers. As you approach the cave, you smell a horrible, musky scent that grows stronger as you get closer.

The cave entrance is completely black, twice as tall as you, and about 10 feet (3 m) wide. The smell is almost overpowering now. What can it be? As you approach the entrance, the ground beneath your feet becomes very soft, and every step you take releases more of the powerful smell. It must be the droppings of some creature . . . maybe birds . . .

Just as you are about to investigate the inside of the cave, you hear shrill squeaking sounds. Something flaps past your head, just missing you. More of the flying creatures swoop past you. Suddenly you are surrounded by thousands of bats! In a panic, you throw yourself against the cave wall, covering your head with your arms. You look up as a great black cloud of bats streams out of the cave. You notice the tiny points of their fangs glistening in the half-light—vampire bats! As they disappear into the evening sky, you shiver. You go in search of shelter elsewhere, afraid they might return to their cave.

Vampire Bats

- Vampire bats live in Central and South America.
- They are only one inch (about 3 cm) long, and weigh as little as 1.7 ounces (50 g).
- These bats drink the blood of large mammals. They feed by making a small cut in the skin with their teeth, then lapping up the blood. They sometimes bite humans.
- Vampire bats do not usually harm the animals they feed from, but some carry a disease called rabies. If you are not vaccinated against rabies and don't receive treatment before symptoms start, you have a very slim chance of survival. See page 79 for more on rabies.
- The saliva of vampire bats contains a substance that stops blood from clotting. This anticoagulant has been used in human medicine to help patients who have had strokes caused by blood clots.

Go to page 18.

You look at the forest floor and shudder. It's alive with crawling things you definitely don't want to share a bed with!

You set to work clearing the ground between two trees, using a stick in case you disturb any snakes. Next, you arrange some fallen logs into a platform, and cut lengths of bamboo with your Swiss Army knife to lay on top of them. You tie a thick bamboo stem between the trees about chest height with liana, which are long vines that make good rope. This is your roof pole. Then you cut more bamboo and lean each stem against the roof pole, tying it with more liana. Finally, you cover it with thick, broad leaves to give you some shelter in case of a downpour. Once inside, you cover yourself with your thin waterproof jacket and close your eyes, trying not to listen to the eerie whoops and shrieks of jungle animals as darkness descends.

Dawn is breaking when a sound wakes you up. You listen intently, peering outside your shelter into the dim light. There it is again! A low, growling sound, and it seems to be coming from the undergrowth just ahead of you.

If you decide to go and investigate the sound, go to page 17.

If you decide to stick your head under your coat and hope the noise goes away, go to page 19.

Rainforest Shelter-building Tips

- Don't sleep or make shelter in these places:
  - near large animal trails (for obvious reasons)
  - on low ground, especially swampy areas, that might be home to mosquitoes, or be likely to flood, which is common in the rainforest.
- Clear a space on the ground to make your shelter. Make sure to do this with a stick, not with your hands, in case there are spiders, snakes, or biting ants.
- Raise your bed off the ground to avoid creepy-crawlies on the forest floor.
- Check above you for rotting branches of dead trees that could fall on you in the night, and any animals that might be lurking in the trees.
- If you have mosquito netting, use it.
- Bamboo is very useful for shelter building, but clumps can easily spring apart and injure you when you cut them. Bamboo splinters are extremely sharp. Be careful!

You tramp onward through the forest with no clear idea of where you're heading. You push through dangling vines, some with sharp thorns that tear at your clothes. Looking up, you see a palm-like tree covered with cascades of juicy, delicious-looking purple berries. Your stomach rumbles loudly, and you realize for the first time how hungry you are.

You have no idea whether the berries are poisonous, but they certainly look tasty.

If you decide to eat some of the berries, go to page 28.

If you decide not to risk it, go to page 34.

You look toward the spot where you thought you heard the sound. You still can't see anything. You decide to creep a bit farther forward, being as quiet as possible, but twigs snap and leaves rustle as you move. You part the branches of a low-growing plant, peering into the greenish gloom of the rainforest at dawn . . .

You think you see movement. Something is there! You look more closely at the spot and almost cry out in fear—a pair of yellow eyes is staring straight at you! You can make out the rest of the animal now—a huge cat, with spotted fur and a long tail—a jaguar. You gulp. The animal snarls, revealing long, pointed teeth. It looks as though it's about to pounce!

If you decide to run away, go to page 24.

If you decide to stand your ground, go to page 26.

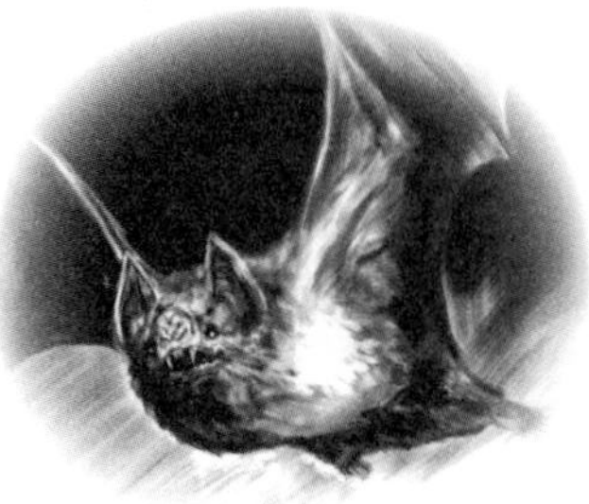

The bat cave has left you feeling out of breath and slightly sick. You can still smell the horrible lingering odor. Through a gap between the treetops, you can see the vampire bats like a dark cloud in the sky. The light is fading fast, and it's becoming difficult to see under the tree canopy. You suddenly feel very tired, and your legs are beginning to ache after so much walking. Then the rain starts. It's so heavy, you feel as though you're standing underneath a shower.

You spot another cave not far away. By now, there's no time for making a shelter to sleep under. Can you face the possibility of another bat colony? Or maybe something more dangerous has made this cave its home. Should you forget the cave and find the strength to carry on walking as night falls around you?

If you decide to risk finding shelter in the new cave, go to page 20.

If you decide to keep walking, go to page 22.

You lie very still, with your head underneath your coat and your eyes squeezed shut. You hear the growling again—it sounds like a large animal! You do your best not to imagine what it looks like, wrap your arms tightly around your body, and pray that the creature—whatever it is—will go away.

After a few moments of silence, you hear rustling in the undergrowth. The animal is finally moving away! You let out a long breath of relief. However, you don't risk moving for another 10 minutes to make sure the animal is far away.

In the dawn light, the rainforest looks gloomy, and you have no way of telling where you are. It occurs to you that you might be better off climbing a tree. Maybe you'll get your bearings that way. On the other hand, the trees are tall and hard to climb and you risk falling.

If you decide to walk, go to page 16.

If you decide to climb a tree, go to page 23.

There's no horrible smell as you approach this cave, and no signs that an animal has been near. Cautiously, you look inside. It's creepy and dark, but it doesn't seem to be inhabited, and it will offer some protection from the rain that is falling fast in fat drops.

You break some leaves off a broad-leafed plant and lay them on the cave floor, placing your waterproof coat on top. Exhausted, you curl up on top of them and drift off to sleep.

You wake up with a start! Did you just hear something? Was that a low, growling sound? There it was again! The hairs on the back of your neck stand up. The sound is terrifying! You stand up, trying to be quiet, and cautiously step outside the cave to investigate.

Looking at the snake's massive body, you realize it must be a constrictor. In your hurry to get away from it, you almost slip and fall from the tree! You realize you're panicking and force yourself to breathe and move as slowly as you can. The snake still hasn't moved. You swing down to the branch below, then look up at the snake—it's still motionless.

Finally you jump down to the forest floor, relieved to be back on the ground again. You walk on through the forest, looking at the ground, mindful of snakes that could be slithering across the forest floor or hiding under fallen leaves.

Go to page 16.

It gets darker as you walk, until you can hardly see anything at all. Sharp thorns stab and tear at you in the darkness and, every few steps, you find yourself stumbling over a tree root or a fallen branch. Mosquitoes whine in your ears. It's still pouring rain, and the ground has become extremely slippery.

You scramble over the trunk of a fallen tree. To your horror, the ground falls away in front of it. You try to grab hold of a branch to stop your fall, but it's dead and snaps off! You hurtle down a steep bank, crashing into trees as you fall, whacking your head on a rock as you tumble down. You lose consciousness . . . and don't wake up again.

The end.

You heave yourself up onto the first branch of a tall tree, then scramble up to a higher one. You look up and see that there is still a very long way to go, and already you're feeling tired in the clammy heat of the rainforest. This is going to be harder than you thought. You're considering whether to abandon the climb, when you catch sight of something that makes you freeze: coiled around a branch in a patch of sunlight, its head two feet (0.5 m) away from you, is an enormous snake.

The snake is well camouflaged against the tree, greenish brown with a spotted pattern. Its body looks thicker than your thigh! The snake's coils wrap around the tree branch—it must be at least twice as long as you are tall. The snake seems to be asleep and doesn't move. Neither do you, as you stand frozen to the spot, deciding what to do . . .

If you decide to step around the snake, and carry on climbing, go to page 30.

If you decide to get down from the tree, go to page 21.

Your heart pounds as you stare, transfixed, into the jaguar's eyes. You scream, turn, and run away as fast as you can through the trees!

It's a matter of seconds before the jaguar catches up with you. It brings you crashing down onto the jungle floor. At the same time, it bites down on your skull with its powerful jaws. You die instantly.

The end.

Jaguars

- It's never a good idea to run away from a large predator such as a big cat. This will make you seem even more like prey, and the animal will almost certainly be able to outrun you.
- Jaguars are South America's biggest cats. They're also found in Central America.
- Jaguars used to be quite common, but are becoming increasingly rare, now found only in remote regions.
- They vary in size, and can weigh from around 100 to 265 pounds (45 to 120 kg). The biggest are nearly seven feet (2 m) long.
- Of all the big cats, jaguars are least likely to attack people —but it has happened.
- They are good swimmers and will eat Amazon River animals such as caimans and turtles.
- A jaguar's jaws deliver the most powerful bite of any big cat in the world. It's even capable of biting through a turtle's shell!

Petrified with fear, you manage to tear your eyes away from the jaguar, in case it interprets your stare as a threat. You look down at the forest floor and keep still. After a few moments, you shrink back behind a tree.

You risk a glance at the animal and see that it hasn't moved and still looks as though it could pounce at any moment. You want to run away, but you know that this will make the big cat more likely to see you as prey and attack. You wait another few moments. Then you cautiously start to back away, very slowly, making sure you are still facing the jaguar. After a while, when you are out of sight of the animal, you hear the big cat moving off in another direction, perhaps in search of easier prey. You've been sweating, and this reminds you that you need to find drinking water.

If you decide to get your water from bamboo, go to page 32.

If you decide to find a river, go to page 34.

If you decide to get your water from a pool in some tree roots, go to page 36.

Finding Water in the Rainforest

You might think this should be pretty easy—after all, this is a rainforest. But finding water might not be as simple as you think.

- Rivers and streams are obvious sources of water. Remember that fast-flowing water is more likely to be good to drink, although it may be more difficult to get to.
- If there are animal tracks around a water source, it's best not to drink from it. As well as drinking the water, the animals might well have used it as a toilet!
- Water can be obtained from bamboo (see page 32).
- You can wait for rain and collect it in a container. Rainwater should be safe to drink without boiling.
- Don't drink directly from any water source because there could be small organisms in it, such as bacteria. There have also been reports of people bending to drink from a pool or river in the Amazon, only to have the tip of their nose nipped off by piranhas!
- Stagnant water should be be avoided. Microscopic parasites and germs breed in it, and it could be home to small creatures you can barely see.
- Digging a hole near a water source and waiting for water to filter up into it will get rid of some of the impurities that might be living in the water. You can also use a piece of cloth as a filter. But it's always worth it to boil water before you drink it (see pages 46–47 for tips on boiling water).

You cut down a huge bunch of the purple fruit, which look like very fat blueberries or black currants. Cautiously, you try one. It's absolutely delicious! Surely nothing this tasty could be poisonous! You sit down on a log and eat until your stomach stops rumbling.

You were foolish to eat a fruit you didn't recognize but, luckily for you, these berries are not poisonous. They are acai berries, one of the thousands of edible fruits of the Amazon, which include figs, pineapples, passion fruit, avocados, and coconuts.

You spot a shrub-like plant not far away. It has round spiky seed cases, a bit like the cases chestnuts grow inside. It has what look like beans inside. Do you still feel hungry? Should you try the new plant, too?

If you decide you're not hungry anymore, go to page 33.

If you still feel hungry and decide to eat the beans, go to page 37.

Testing Fruits for Poison

Instead of gorging yourself on the berries and hoping for the best, you should have tested for poison in a much more careful and scientific way.

- Don't eat any plant that has mildew on it.
- Crush the fruit and sniff it. If it smells like almonds or peaches, don't eat it!
- To be on the safe side, don't eat any plant with white sap because many of them are poisonous.
- Put some juice on your skin. If it irritates your skin, don't eat it.
- Try a tiny amount of juice on your lips. If it tingles or feels sore or unusual in any way, don't eat the fruit.
- Try a little juice in the corner of your mouth and wait for any reaction. Then try some on your tongue, then under your tongue. Finally, chew a small piece then spit it out. Wait a few minutes between each stage to make sure you don't have a reaction.
- If the fruit has passed all of the above tests, swallow a small piece of it. Wait several hours, without eating or drinking anything else. If you feel fine, then the fruit is safe to eat.
- Remember that you've only tested one part of the plant. The stems, leaves, and roots might not be safe to eat and will need to be tested, too.
- Remember, these tests aren't foolproof!

Cautiously, you place one foot slightly closer to the snake to climb up to a higher branch. The snake opens its huge jaws, lunges toward you, then retreats very quickly. In a panic, you slip and fall, grabbing onto the branch closest to the snake.

The snake lunges for you again and, this time, it bites! You feel its sharp teeth holding you firmly and painfully by the shoulder. Quickly and purposefully, its body uncoils from the branch and wraps around your body. You feel it start to squeeze . . .

Unfortunately for you, the snake is a constrictor, a green anaconda that kills its prey by squeezing it tighter and tighter until it can no longer breathe. You are soon dead.

The end.

Green Anacondas

- The green anaconda is the biggest snake in the world and can measure up to 30 feet (9 m) long and weigh up to 500 pounds (230 kg)!
- Like other constricting snakes, such as pythons, anacondas don't have venom. They kill their prey by coiling around it and squeezing until the animal can't breathe.
- Green anacondas are good swimmers and live near water. Like crocodiles, they can lie in wait for prey in water with just their eyes and nostrils above the surface.
- Anacondas prey on fish, birds, capybaras, turtles, caimans, deer, and wild pigs. They can even eat large animals whole because their jaws can stretch wide open. After a big meal, they might not eat again for months!
- Reticulated pythons, found in Southeast Asia, can be even longer than green anacondas, but their bodies aren't as thick and heavy.
- Although large anacondas are capable of eating an animal the size of a human, there are very few reports of the creatures attacking people, and no records of fatal attacks.

There's a stand of bamboo not far away. Luckily, you know just how to get water from it.

Tap the bamboo stems—the ones that sound denser are likely to have water in them. You might even be able to hear the water sloshing around if you shake the stem.

Cut the stem and collect the water in a container. It should be safe to drink but, if you want to be extra careful, you should boil it. You need to be careful when you make your cut in the bamboo stem because split bamboo can be extremely sharp.

You drink until you're no longer thirsty.

Go to page 38.

Something glints on the forest floor ahead of you. As you get closer, you see it's a pool of water, like a very large puddle, but it seems to be quite deep. You're hot and clammy, and the pool looks so inviting. It's also a good opportunity for a much-needed wash.

If you decide to take a dip in the pool, go to page 62.

If you decide to keep going, go to page 45.

You walk for half an hour or so. Ahead of you, through the trees, it's getting brighter and brighter. It's not long before you hear the sound of moving water.

When you find the water's edge, it's as though a light has been switched on! After the gloom of the thick tree canopy, you blink bleary eyed in the light. The river is wide and slow moving here at the edge, but it's moving swiftly along in the middle. This must be either the Amazon River itself or one of its many large tributaries.

Go to page 46.

Amazing Amazon River

- The Amazon is the world's largest river by volume. It's in competition with Africa's Nile River for the World's Longest River record. This depends on how you measure where the river begins and ends, and there's a lot of argument about it. The Amazon is at least 3,852 miles (6,200 km) long. It starts as a trickle in the Andes Mountains of Peru and flows across South America all the way to the Atlantic Ocean.
- The mouth of the Amazon, where it flows into the Atlantic, is 200 miles (322 km) wide. Even if you travel more than 930 miles (1,500 km)—upstream (that's more than the distance between London and Rome!)—it's still more than six miles (10 km) wide.
- There are no bridges across the Amazon at any point. It's either too wide or in the middle of the rainforest. You'll have to swim or raft across it.
- Every second, 55 million gallons (208,000 cu meters) pour into the Atlantic Ocean from the Amazon River.
- The Amazon River has more than 1,000 tributaries. Seventeen of them are longer than 930 miles (1,500 km), making them some of the longest rivers in the world.
- More species of fish live in the Amazon than in any other body of water on Earth!
- Most people of the Amazon live near a river. If you follow a river downstream for long enough, you should find people.
- The largest city along the Amazon River is Manaus, in Brazil, and it is home to 1.7 million people.

The tangled roots of a huge tree wind around one another at the tree's base to make what looks like an enormous bird's nest. There are plenty of small pools of water among them. You cup a handful of water. It looks clear and smells fresh. Surely it can only be rainwater?

You're very thirsty and don't have any easy way of making a fire. You could go about the laborious process of hunting for dry wood, making a fire and boiling the water (see pages 46–47), but this will take some time and slow you down in your quest to find help. Or you could just drink some. It looks very tempting, and you're in dire need of a drink.

If you decide to boil the water, go to page 38.

If you decide to risk it and drink the water without boiling it, go to page 40.

You collect a couple of handfuls of the beans and eat them. Unfortunately, you have just made a BIG mistake. This is a castor oil plant. Its seeds, which look like beans, contain a lethal toxin called ricin.

You carry on walking through the forest but, after a couple of hours, you start to feel burning in your mouth and throat. You have to stop. Your stomach hurts, you feel increasingly weak, and you get diarrhea. You're dead within a few days.

The end.

You feel refreshed after your drink of clean water. But your stomach is rumbling, and you spot a plant you think you recognize.

There's more light where a large tree has fallen, creating a gap in the tree canopy, and there are lots of smaller shrubs growing there, taking advantage of the light. One of them is a small tree with oval-shaped fruits hanging from it. Some of the fruit is orangey-yellow, some green. You are almost sure these are papayas, or pawpaws.

But you're in the middle of the Amazon Rainforest, not your local supermarket! Could these be poisonous fruit that look very similar to papayas?

Using your Swiss Army knife, you cut open the orange fruit. Inside, the golden flesh smells delicious and leaves your mouth watering. There are black seeds in the middle. This is just how you remember papayas.

It's a dilemma. You're starting to feel weak with hunger, you haven't seen any other edible plants that you recognize, and you're pretty convinced that these fruits are safe. On the other hand, you haven't eaten papaya very often. Is it possible you're just convincing yourself that this fruit is the same because you're so very hungry?

If you decide not to eat the fruit, go to page 44.

If you decide to eat the fruit, go to page 49.

Surviving Without Food or Water

As long as you have enough water to drink, you can survive without food for quite a long time—probably a month or more. But how long depends on different factors:

- Some people use up energy more quickly than others, so this will make a difference to how long you can survive without eating. It will also depend on how much physical work you're doing.
- If you're strong, fit, and healthy, and neither very old nor very young, you'll survive longer.
- Carrying a bit of excess fat will be an advantage, too, as the extra fat on your body can be used as fuel.

Surviving without water is entirely different. Certain factors make a difference. It will depend on how fit you are, the temperature, which is generally pretty hot in the Amazon, and how much exercise you're doing. However, you won't survive for long without a drink whatever the circumstances. After three days without water, you'll be in serious danger of death, and it might be sooner than that if you're hot and working hard.

Haven't you been paying any attention at all? It's never a good idea to drink stagnant water!

Tiny parasites and bacteria can thrive in pools of stagnant water, like the one you have very foolishly drunk from without boiling first. Water-borne diseases include typhoid, Weil's disease, and schistomiasis, or snail fever.

Unfortunately, you now have cholera from the contaminated water. You continue on your journey through the rainforest for a while, but it isn't long before you start to feel ill. Soon you have terrible diarrhea and vomiting. You're unable to find enough water to replace the liquids you're losing. With no chance of getting medical help, you die.

The end.

You start walking downstream. From the corner of your eye, you think you spot movement by the water's edge. But when you look, nothing is there. There's a soft splash, and you turn to see bubbles in the water near the shore. What creature might have made them? A prickle of fear runs down your spine, and you start to feel very glad you didn't take a dip!

The water's making you so jumpy that you wonder if you should get away from the river and go back into the jungle instead.

If you decide to get away from the water's edge, go to page 68.

If you decide to continue walking by the river, go to page 74.

You lie in wait again, staring into the water with your spear poised in midair. Minutes pass and your arm begins to ache.

After half an hour of gazing into the murky water, you decide to wade in and see if you have better luck that way. You try the bottom with your spear. It's pretty shallow. You wade into the water, your spear in your hand, ready for the first sign of a fish.

Electric eels are common in these waters. They're difficult to see in muddy water and, unfortunately, you come into contact with a big one. It releases a huge electric current, and you fall into the water. You are dead within moments.

The end.

Electric Eels

- Electric eels are common in the Amazon and Orinoco rivers, as well as in their tributaries and swamps. They prefer very slow-moving, murky water.
- Although they're called eels and they look like eels, electric eels are more closely related to catfish.
- They can be large, growing up to eight feet (2.5 m) long and weighing 45 pounds (20 kg).
- The eels eat fish that they find with their electrical receptors and stun with an electric current. They also use electricity to warn off large predators.
- The current they produce can be as much as 600 volts. An electric socket carries 120 volts!
- Electric eels can even produce an electrical charge when they're dead.

You decide not to eat the fruit, just in case. But, as far as you know, there are no poisonous fish in the Amazon. You could try to catch one and eat that. On the other hand, it might not be worth the energy you use up, especially if you only end up catching a tiny fish. After all, you know you can go without food for a very long time before it becomes life-threatening.

If you decide not to bother, go to page 54.

If you decide to try fishing, go to page 64.

You carry on walking, still hot and sweaty and covered in insect bites. There are mosquitoes and flies that bite during the day and at night. You hope none of them has given you a disease.

A dip would have been refreshing, but maybe a river is a better bet, and there must be one not far away—after all, this is the Amazon! It isn't long before you hear the sound of trickling water and find a stream. You follow it downstream and hope that eventually, it will lead to a river.

Go to page 34.

You collect some water from the river in your salvaged metal container and set about making a fire. Once the water's been boiling for a few minutes, you reckon it'll be safe to drink. You leave it to cool for a bit, then drink thirstily.

You feel better, but you're still very hot and sweaty. A quick dip in the river is tempting—but what creatures might be lurking in there?

If you decide not to swim, go to page 41.

If you decide to swim, go to page 50.

Making a Fire

Boiling water will kill most disease-causing bacteria. Here are some tips for making a fire in the rainforest.

- The forest floor will be damp, so arrange some stones to build your fire on. Make sure they're not really wet (for example, stones from a stream), because wet stones can explode in a fire!
- You need tinder to start your fire. This is very dry material that catches fire easily. In the rainforest, it's hard to find. Try fine wood shavings, cotton cloth or cotton balls, bark, or the insides of birds' nests. You might need to leave your tinder in the sunshine to dry out completely. Good tinder needs only a spark to make it catch fire.
- Arrange a pyramid of kindling, or small, dry twigs around your tinder. If the outside of the twig is damp, cut it back until you reach dry wood.
- You need something that will make a spark. If you don't have matches, focus sunlight through a lens such as a glass bottle, a magnifying glass, or a pair of glasses, to make a bright spot of light on your tinder. Blow on it very gently as it starts to glow.
- Once your kindling is burning well, add small pieces of dry wood. When the fire is hotter, you can use wood that's a bit damp. It'll be smoky, but that will keep biting insects away.

Your wound throbs as you walk, so you take it slowly. It's not bleeding anymore. You only hope it isn't infected.

A squawk makes you jump, and you look up to see a parrot high up in the trees. You stop to watch the beautiful red-and-blue bird as it swoops away. As you follow its direction, you realize you were right—it does look brighter that way. You keep going, feeling optimistic.

Go to page 34.

You've taken a chance . . . and luckily the fruit is papaya, just like you thought, and it's safe to eat. You feel much better after eating the ripe, juicy flesh and the peppery-tasting seeds. You've been lucky this time, but it's not a good idea to eat anything in the rainforest unless you are 100% sure of what it is.

Although it's not as good as actually drinking clean water, the juicy fruit will help to keep you hydrated, too. With this in mind, you consider picking some more fruit to take with you. It might be heavy and awkward to carry, though, and the jungle seems to be full of edible plants. Then again, you spot a different kind of fruit that's within reach around the other side of the tree.

If you decide to continue your journey without picking any fruit, go to page 55.

If you decide to pick some more fruit, go to page 58.

You take off your clothes, wash them in the river, and leave them hanging on a branch to dry. Then you wade into the water. It feels wonderful on your hot, clammy skin as you swim not too far from the shore.

Lots of people regularly swim in the Amazon. But you're very unlucky, because you accidentally wake up an enormous black caiman that is sleeping on the riverbed. These animals usually hunt at night, but this one is hungry and loses no time in drowning you, then eating an easy meal.

The end.

Amazon River Creatures

As well as the black caiman that just had you for breakfast (see page 75), the rivers and swamps of the Amazon are home to many types of fish and mammals.

- The world's largest freshwater fish, the pirarucu, lives in the Amazon. It's enormous—from six to thirteen feet (2 to 4 m) long—and is unusual because it breathes air. Pirarucus feed on other fish and have teeth on their tongues and the roofs of their mouths.
- You're more likely to meet a spectacled caiman than a potentially dangerous black caiman. They are more common, lighter in color, and smaller. But they can still give you a nasty bite if you step on one by accident.
- Pink river dolphins are freshwater mammals that live in the Amazon and Orinoco river systems, feeding on fish and crabs. They have long, thin snouts and are pale pink in color. Males can be up to nine feet (2.7 m) long and 300 pounds (136 kg).
- The mata mata turtle is one of the strangest-looking animals of the Amazon! It has a flat, triangular head covered in bumps and flaps of skin, and a long, thin snout. It's well camouflaged and looks a bit like tree bark or a clump of fallen leaves. It lies in wait to ambush fish and other small creatures.
- The largest aquatic mammal of the Amazon is the huge manatee (see page 101).

You try not to panic as you think about how to find water to wash your wound. There must be a stream not far away. You blunder off in search of one, bleeding heavily and dragging your wounded leg.

Eventually, you do find a fast-running stream, and the water does seem clean enough. But, by this time, you've lost a lot of blood. As you approach the stream, you realize you're too weak to wash your wound. You slump down on the forest floor and pass out, never to regain consciousness.

The end.

Health and First Aid

- If you're injured and the wound is bleeding a lot, the most important thing to do is stop the bleeding. An average adult has about 10 pints (4.7 L) of blood. Losing one to two pints (0.5 to 1 L) of blood will make an adult feel faint; losing about five pints (2.4 L) can cause death.
- To stop a wound from bleeding, apply pressure with a bandage or whatever material you have. But be careful not to tie it too tightly or you could cut off the blood flow to the wound and end up doing more damage.
- Open wounds are a serious risk of infection in the rainforest's damp, warm conditions. There are lots of biting insects and bacteria breeds quickly. It's important to keep wounds clean.
- Even if you're not wounded, keeping clean is vital in the jungle. For example, potentially fatal Chagas disease is transmitted by a blood-sucking insect that leaves droppings next to where it has punctured the skin. If you scratch the wound without cleaning it first, you'll become infected with the disease.

Your stomach growls as you trudge onward, but you ignore it. You know that you can survive a long time without eating, and you decide it's not worth the risk just to stop a rumbling stomach.

Go to page 61.

You're feeling refreshed after eating the fruit, but your feet hurt as you walk. Soon they become so painful that you have to stop. You sit on a log and take off your shoes and socks. The bottoms of your feet are white and wrinkled, and painful to touch.

If you decide to stop and rest to try to heal your feet, go to page 69.

If you decide to walk through the pain and find help as quickly as possible, go to page 90.

You walk along the trail, keeping an eye out for signs that humans might have come this way. You don't see any but, after awhile, you sense something else—a terrible smell, like rotting garbage, with a hint of burnt rubber. The smell gets worse and now you hear a rumbling noise as well as barking. Maybe it's people with their hunting dogs, you think hopefully. Suddenly there are what seems like hundreds of hairy pig-like animals hurtling toward you. Your wound makes it difficult for you to get out of the way of the creatures quickly enough. To make matters worse, you stagger and fall against one of the babies, and it squeals! Chattering their huge, tusk-like teeth and barking, two of the animals attack you!

The animals' tusks are sharp, and they attack viciously. You are already wounded and weak and, by the time the animals leave, you have lost a lot of blood. You sink to the forest floor, bleeding uncontrollably.

The end.

White-lipped Peccaries

The herd of animals you encountered were white-lipped peccaries.

- Found throughout most of Central and South America, peccaries look like pigs with long snouts for rooting. But, in fact, they are not related to pigs.
- White-lipped peccaries are dark brown or black and are covered in bristly hairs. They grow up to about four feet (1.2 m) long and weigh up to 90 pounds (40 kg).
- They live in herds of at least 20 animals, but can number several hundred! They make barking sounds and, when they're threatened, they chatter their teeth.
- They give off a strong smell, similar to the smell of a skunk, which comes from scent glands on their backs. The smell helps the herd members identify one another.
- White-lipped peccaries are the largest and most aggressive peccary species. They often attack and kill dogs, but they're very rarely dangerous to humans.

In your eagerness to collect the fruit from the tree, you've forgotten to check the ground. You're not the only one attracted by the fruit! So are different small mammals which, in turn, attract . . . snakes!

The one you've just walked into is well camouflaged on the forest floor and is highly venomous—a bushmaster. Alarmed, it strikes at your leg, delivering a lethal dose of venom. Your leg begins to swell rapidly. You vomit and have severe diarrhea, stabbing pains, then numbness. After 40 minutes, you lose consciousness and you soon die.

The end.

Bushmaster Snake

- Bushmasters are one of the world's most venomous snakes. They are found in Central and South America, especially in the Amazon Rainforest.
- Bushmasters are a type of pit viper. These are snakes that have heat-sensitive pits on their heads, which they use to detect small animals for prey.
- They're the longest venomous snake in the Americas and can grow up to 12 feet (3.7 m) long, though on average they're less than six feet (1.8 m).
- Bushmasters are reddish brown in color, with an irregular diamond-shaped pattern along their thick bodies. This means they're well camouflaged on the rainforest floor.
- The snakes are rarely seen, partly because of their camouflage and partly because they are usually nocturnal.
- Bushmasters can be aggressive, especially if they're startled. They have been known to bite and kill people.

You rip a strip of cloth from your shirt and gingerly apply it to the wound, tying it in place firmly but not too tightly. Your makeshift bandage provides enough pressure to stop the bleeding. You rest for awhile, then cautiously stand up and move. The wound is painful, but at least it's not pouring with blood. There's even more reason for you to find help now so, despite the pain, you carry on.

There's a well-worn trail ahead of you, possibly made by animals, but you hope it might be made by people. Instead, you could meander through the trees. You're not sure which route to take, but it does look a little bit brighter as you look through the trees in the opposite direction from the trail. Maybe there's a river that way.

If you decide to walk through the trees, go to page 48.

If you decide to take the trail, go to page 56.

As you pass a hollow tree, you hear a buzzing sound. There are a few bees near the tree and as you take a closer look, you can see that bees have made their home inside the hollow trunk. You know that honey is one of the most nutritious, easy-to-digest, energy-giving foods you could possibly find. And honeycomb will last a long time, too. It might be worth a few stings to get to the precious honey. If it proves too difficult, you can always walk away again. After all, you know you're not allergic to bee stings.

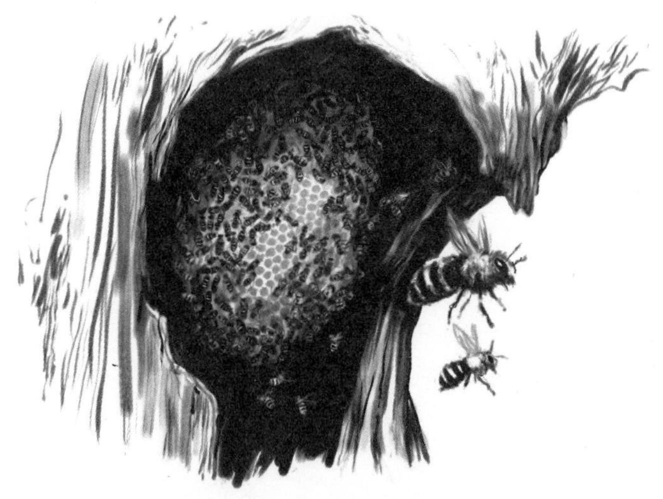

If you decide to try to take some honey from the beehive, go to page 66.

If you decide not to risk getting stung, go to page 73.

The water does feel good as you step into it. But soon after that, it begins to feel very, very bad.

You feel a sharp, tearing pain in your leg and cry out, then another–something is biting you! You lunge for the side of the pool and scramble out, shaking. There are two very nasty bites on your leg, and you can see that whole chunks of flesh are missing! You've been bitten by hungry, red-bellied piranhas, which must have been trapped in the pool during a flood and become stranded there.

You feel sick as you look down at your bleeding wounds and try to decide what to do. You're bleeding heavily. What should you do? You could make a bandage from your clothing, but your clothes are very far from being sterile, and you might end up causing a fatal infection. Or you could try to find some clean water to wash the wounds.

If you decide to go in search of clean water, go to page 52.

If you decide to apply a bandage, go to page 60.

Piranhas

- Piranhas are found in lakes and rivers in South America and are quite common.
- There are lots of different types. Some are even vegetarian! The most ferocious is the meat-eating red-bellied piranha, which weighs up to eight pounds (3.5 kg), measures up to 13 inches (33 cm), and has the strongest jaws.
- Piranha teeth are razor sharp. To keep them that way, the teeth are replaced throughout the fish's life.
- Red-bellied piranhas prey on fish, worms, and other small animals.
- Usually, they leave large animals alone, although they sometimes bite and can be very dangerous if they've become trapped in a pool left by flooding.
- The terrifying reputation of piranhas is partly due to American President Theodore Roosevelt, who wrote a book about his travels, in which he described piranhas as "the embodiment of evil ferocity" and claimed they would eat cattle alive if they stepped into the water. They aren't quite as bad as that, although they are responsible for taking the odd chunk out of people, not to mention fingers and toes.

You find a stick about twice the length of your arm, and a vine with long, sharp thorns. Carefully, you break off some of the thorns and tie them to the stick, using the vine as string. You now have a spear with several sharp tips.

You lie on the bank, peering into the slow-moving, murky water with the spear in your hand, ready to strike. You make out a dark shape and stab down with your spear—you've caught a fish! It's not very big, but it's a good start. You make a fire and cook the fish (see pages 46-47). It's delicious. Should you stay and catch more fish, or move on?

If you decide to stay and catch another fish, go to page 42.

If you decide to move on, go to page 61.

Fishing in the Amazon

- Kneel or sit down, to hide yourself from the fish. Make sure you don't let your shadow fall on the surface of the water.
- If you're experienced at fishing with a hook and line, you should try it. Make hooks from thorns and use liana for your line.
- If you are not experienced, tie something heavy to one end of a length of liana, and tie the other end firmly to the bank. Bait thorns with worms and attach them to the liana at intervals. Drop the weighted end into the water and leave it for a while—maybe overnight—before bringing in the line. Hopefully fish will be attached.
- Make a trap that fish can swim into but can't easily get out of. For example, use a plastic bottle with the top section cut off, turned around, and placed back inside the bottle so that the bottle top is facing inward into the bottom of the bottle.
- "Tickling" fish takes a lot of practice: put your hand into the water under the bank and wait. When you feel a fish, gently move your fingers along its belly, then grab it and pull it out quickly.
- Spear a fish using a stick with sharp thorns attached.
- Never eat a dead fish you find floating on the surface of the water. It could be diseased or rotten.
- Remember there are dangers lurking in the waters of the Amazon: electric eels can electrocute you, piranhas can give you a nasty bite, and a large enough caiman could eat you!

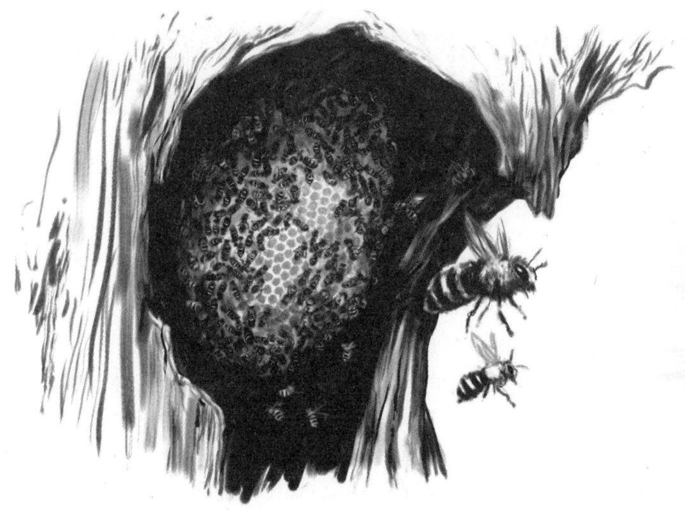

You take a step toward the hive and, immediately, several bees land on you and sting. You swat at them. Within seconds, you're surrounded by a cloud of stinging bees. You run away, but there are bees already on you and hundreds more in hot pursuit. So many bees have stung you that, even though you're not allergic to bee stings, you have a heart attack and die.

The end.

Africanized Honeybees

- Believe it or not, Africanized honeybees are more feared by people in the Amazon than anacondas, jaguars, snakes, or spiders!
- The bees were introduced by accident in the 1950s by scientists who had crossed European honeybees with African honeybees. They're now widespread in South America, Central America, and the southern United States.
- They are more aggressive than European honeybees and will defend their hive ferociously. When one bee stings, it releases a chemical alerting other bees to the threat which causes them to sting, too.
- The sting of an Africanized honeybee is no more toxic or painful than a European honeybee's sting, but the danger is that lots of bees will sting at once. If you're stung enough times, you'll die.
- Some people are allergic to bee stings and could die from even one sting from a regular honeybee.
- The Africanized bees, also known as killer bees, are out-competing native Amazonian bees, which are mostly stingless.

There's a trail leading from the riverside back into the forest, and you take it. You realize you might be heading into a different danger, but you couldn't stand being beside the river any longer. You're sure there was something lurking there.

The farther you walk from the river, the gloomier it gets. You start to wonder if you'd be better off going back . . . when suddenly you hear movement in the trees and whirl around, your heart pounding. There's a snorting sound. Could it be something fierce, like a jaguar? You draw in a breath and hide behind a tree. But you breathe out again when you see what's making the sounds. Not far away, a tapir snuffles around on the forest floor. It stops and stares at you in alarm, then runs off. What a relief!

The trail splits in two. One leads deeper into the forest, while the other looks as though it will take you back to the river, farther downstream.

If you decide to take the trail back toward the river, go to page 77.

If you decide to go deeper into the forest, go to page 72.

You find a stream and rinse out your drenched, sweaty socks, then hang them to dry in a patch of sunlight, thankful that it isn't raining. You clean your feet, too, as best you can. You push a couple of sturdy sticks into the forest floor, then hang your wet boots from them, facing downward. That way, nothing is likely to crawl into them! You spread your waterproof jacket out on the floor in the sunshine and sit on it so that your feet are in the sun and the rest of you is in the shade. Before long, your feet start to feel slightly better.

You've made the right decision. Your feet are showing the first signs of warm water immersion foot, a consequence of continuously keeping your feet in warm and wet conditions. You rest while your socks and boots dry out, then put them on again. Your feet still hurt, but not nearly as much.

A strange chirping sound makes you investigate some tree roots. In a small pool of water among the roots, there's a tiny, bright-blue frog. It's beautiful! You've never seen anything like it before.

If you decide it's time you were moving on, go to page 73.

If you decide to stay and observe the tree frog, and maybe give your feet a longer breather, go to page 86.

You don't want to alarm the sloth, just get a better look. But as you approach, the creature lashes out with its long, filthy-looking claws, then takes a savage bite out of your hand, which you're holding up to it as you would to a dog.

You stagger backward, shocked. You thought sloths barely moved, and you had no idea they were dangerous! The sloth has made deep wounds in your arms and face with its long claws, and they're pouring with blood. You can hardly bear to look at the nasty wound in your hand. Now that the shock is wearing off, the pain is kicking in, making you feel sick. You look at the sloth, which is still hanging upside down in the tree. It looks absolutely filthy. Who knows what bacteria are lurking in those claws? You decide you have to find water to clean the dirty wounds, so you lurch off in search of some. However, it's not long before the blood loss makes you pass out. Without shelter, water, and medical attention, you soon die.

The end.

Sloths

- There are two-toed sloths and three-toed sloths, named for the number of claws on their front paws. Two-toed sloths are bigger and more aggressive and range from 18 to 34 inches (46 to 86 cm) long and 20 pounds (nine kg) in weight.
- Sloths are the world's slowest mammals. They spend 70% of their time resting and are only active for about two hours a day.
- Although they look a bit like monkeys, sloths are related to anteaters. They are found in Central and South America.
- They spend almost all their time hanging upside down in trees—they even give birth that way! They're very clumsy on land and have to pull themselves along with their claws.
- Sloths have been falsely accused of sleeping up to 20 hours a day. In fact, they only sleep for about ten. However, even when they are awake, they don't move very much.
- Because they don't move around much, algae sometimes grows on sloths' fur, which makes them appear green in color, even though their fur is actually brown. Moths sometimes live in their fur, too!
- Sloths eat leaves and fruit, and sometimes feed on plants other animals can't eat, thanks to special bacteria in their stomachs.
- A sloth's claws can be up to four inches (10 cm) long, although they aren't especially sharp. Sloths can and do scratch and bite if they feel threatened.

You keep trudging onward along the rough trail, tapping the ground in front of you with a stick in case there's a snake under the leaf mold, when you spot movement from the corner of your eye. You stop and look; it's another tapir—or maybe the same one. You watch it for a moment as it roots around on the ground. Then it occurs to you that this might be a good hunting opportunity. The tapir isn't very big and looks quite gentle. Plus, you've heard they're very tasty! Eating some nutritious meat will be good for you. On the other hand, hunting's not for the squeamish!

If you decide not to hunt the tapir, go to page 76.

If you decide to hunt the animal, go to page 89.

You hear a crashing sound high above you in the tree canopy. Looking up, you catch sight of movement in the trees. It's a group of big, black-and-brown monkeys. There must be around 10 of them swinging through the trees! You can see they have long tails that grab the branches like extra arms.

It occurs to you that these monkeys have similar needs to yours in terms of food and water. Perhaps you should follow them. On the other hand, you've heard that monkeys can be dangerous. They've stopped in the trees above you, and you look up to see they are watching you!

If you decide to try to follow the monkeys in search of food and water, go to page 78.

If you decide to observe them while they're here, but continue on your way, go to page 96.

If you're frightened of a monkey attack and run away, go to page 98.

You should have trusted your instincts . . .

The splash you heard and the ripples you saw were caused by one of the biggest animals in the Amazon Rainforest–a black caiman, the largest member of the alligator family. This is an especially big male, and it weighs around eight times as much as you do. These creatures often hunt animals at the water's edge, such as capybaras which are enormous rodents. Although they usually hunt at night, this one is active now, and he's spotted you as you stop to take a breather at the water's edge. He takes his opportunity, lunging from the water, grabbing you, and dragging you down underneath the surface to drown.

Look on the bright side: at least it's all over pretty quickly.

The end.

Black Caimans

- Black caimans are big! They grow up to 16 feet (five m) long and can weight up to 880 pounds (400 kg).
- They are mainly nocturnal, and their dark coloring helps to camouflage them at night.
- They prey on fish and on mammals at the water's edge such as capybaras, which are a bit like giant guinea pigs and are the world's biggest rodents.
- There have been a few human deaths caused by black caimans, but the location of their habitat means that they don't often come into contact with people.
- Humans hunted black caimans until they nearly died out. Black caimans are now protected, but some people still hunt them illegally for their leather and meat.

You're on the lookout for other creatures as you continue. Every so often, there's a high-pitched cry, a squawk, or a hoot! You're almost used to the sounds of the rainforest now. But it's a constant reminder that the place is full of life. As well as the tapirs you've just seen, there are probably countless other animals that you can't see, camouflaged in the rainforest.

You're passing underneath a tree when something makes you look up. You find yourself staring straight into a sad-eyed, upside-down face. The creature's scruffy brown fur is tinged with green, and it hangs from the tree from its long, hairy arms and legs. You realize this creature is a sloth.

The creature has one of the cutest faces you've ever seen. But should you be alarmed? Are sloths dangerous?

If you decide sloths are harmless, go to page 70.

If you decide to run away, go to page 81.

You keep your eye on the water, looking for the signs that gave you the unsettling feeling earlier on. But it doesn't look as though there's anything in the water here.

Feeling less worried about the river, you carry on along the trail, which becomes narrower and narrower. Eventually, it ends. What now? You don't want to go back into the forest. The river itself should be a lot easier to navigate, and faster, too. You could spend some time making a raft. Or you could just swim for it, letting the current carry you. After all, you've heard that someone once swam the entire length of the Amazon River!

If you decide to swim, go to page 80.

If you decide to make a raft, go to page 84.

You soon realize it's going to be impossible to follow the monkeys. When they move, they move fast! But one of the monkeys is acting oddly. It starts to make an eerie howling cry and suddenly comes crashing down from the trees toward you!

These are howler monkeys, which are not usually aggressive toward people. However, you have been extremely unlucky, because this particular howler monkey has been infected with rabies, possibly from a vampire bat (see page 13). The disease is making him behave aggressively. The monkey swings down from a tree in front of you, delivers a vicious bite, then quickly swings off.

The bite is painful but, far worse, you are now infected with rabies. It takes a while, but because you're far away from medical help, you die of the disease.

The end.

Howler Monkeys

- Howler monkeys are the largest monkeys in the Americas. They can be up to three feet (1 m) tall, with a tail the same length, and weigh up to about 22 pounds (10 kg).
- They are also the loudest monkeys and one of the loudest animals in the world! Male howler monkeys have a special voice box, which they use to make a guttural cry that can be heard over two miles (5 km) away. They howl at dawn and dusk to warn other troops of howler monkeys that this is their territory. There are 15 different species of howler monkeys.
- The monkeys tend to stay up in the treetops and are active during the day. They eat leaves, fruit, and flowers.
- Howler monkeys, like the many other species of monkeys in the Amazon, are not usually dangerous to humans.

Rabies

Rabies is most commonly transmitted by bats, dogs, and monkeys. The disease has some horrible symptoms. If it's not treated early, it is fatal . . .

- A few weeks after being bitten, you feel pain around the cut. During the next few days, you start to feel anxious and sensitive to light and loud noises.
- Within another week or so, you find it increasingly difficult to swallow and become afraid of water. You become more and more paranoid and start to hallucinate.
- You find it very difficult to swallow saliva, and have periods of thrashing wildly, biting, and spitting.
- Soon you are completely paralyzed, fall into a coma, and die.

It is true that someone swam 3,273 miles (5,268 km) along the Amazon! It was record-breaking marathon swimmer Martin Strel in 2007, but he probably wasn't as weak, exhausted, and covered in insect bites as you are. Your swim starts off fine but, as you move into the middle of the river, the current is just too strong for you, and you struggle for air in the churning water. You bash your head painfully on a piece of driftwood, swallow too much water, and drown.

Maybe it would have been better to build a raft after all.

The end.

You've been lost in the rainforest for a while now, but you're no closer to finding help. It must make sense to find a river, because you know that's where the people of the Amazon are most likely to live. You decide to make it your priority, once you find it, you'll make a raft and float downstream. Eventually, you'll find help that way.

It's not long before you hear the trickle of water—a stream! You tramp alongside it and follow it downstream as it widens and flows into a bigger stream. You follow this until it joins a wide river.

Go to page 84.

The sun beats down as you glide through the water. You're very hot, but you're making such good progress that you're glad you didn't bother stopping. Your skin is covered by your clothes, so you figure you won't get sunburned.

After awhile, you start to feel sick and faint. You're sweating more than ever. You become dizzy, and you realize you should stop and try to find some water to drink. But you're just too tired and confused.

You're suffering from heatstroke, and it's not long before you lose consciousness. With no one to help you, you don't wake up again.

The end.

Heatstroke

- Heat exhaustion, which can make you feel faint and sick, occurs when the body temperature rises above its normal 98°F to 104°F (37°C to 40°C). If it's left untreated, it can become heatstroke.
- You have heatstroke at a body temperature above 104°F (40°C). It is extremely serious (as you have just found out).
- The body overheats and dehydrates, its cells break down, and its organs can no longer work properly.
- Symptoms include rapid, shallow breathing, confusion, heavy sweating that suddenly stops (because there's no more water in the body), and loss of consciousness.
- If heatstroke isn't treated, it can lead to organ failure, brain damage, and death.
- Treatment involves cooling the patient and giving them plenty of water or sports drinks. Avoid anything with caffeine in it.

You look around for things that might help you make a raft. Not far away, there's a stand of bamboo—one of the most useful plants in the rainforest. Because the stems are hollow, they float well. You manage to cut enough thick stems to make a raft. You lie them down side by side and tie them together securely with lengths of liana.

You push your raft into the water—it floats! Cautiously, you climb aboard. You're still afloat! You find a long, strong stick to help you push off from the side and help you steer, then get back onto the raft and push with your pole out into the middle of the river.

Go to page 88.

Making a Raft

- You can build a raft from anything that will float—logs, oil cans, even empty bottles and cans. Bamboo is a perfect raft-making material because it's so buoyant. Balsa wood, which also grows in the Amazon, is another good material for making a raft because it's extremely light. Amazon tribespeople often make canoes out of balsa.

- Your design can be as simple or as complicated as you like. The important thing is that it floats! In a survival situation, the simpler the better. But ideally, you should attach some poles across the underside of the raft to make it sturdy. Attach the poles at right angles to the base of the raft.

- Don't forget that you need to build your raft either right next to the water's edge, or actually in the water. You don't want to have to carry or drag a heavy structure across the forest floor.

You can't resist picking up the cute little frog, which is no bigger than your thumb. But that turns out to have been a very bad idea!

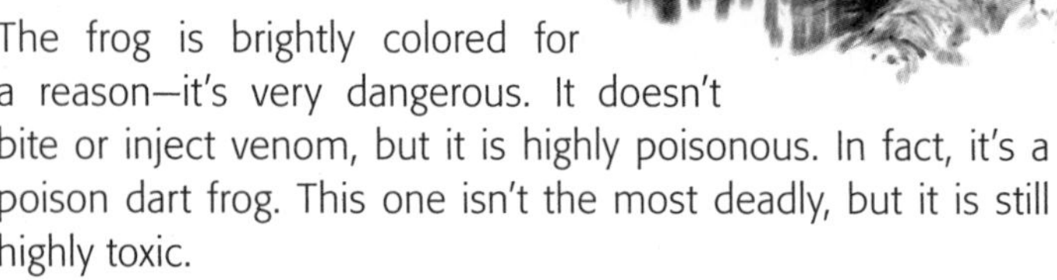

The frog is brightly colored for a reason—it's very dangerous. It doesn't bite or inject venom, but it is highly poisonous. In fact, it's a poison dart frog. This one isn't the most deadly, but it is still highly toxic.

You are blissfully unaware of this and, after studying the little frog, which hops about on your hand for a bit, you gently return it to its tree-root home.

Unfortunately, the frog's poison is entering your bloodstream through the various tiny cuts and insect bites on your hands. And because you don't know that the creature could be poisonous, you're not being careful about hygiene. When you get another cut on your hand from a thorny vine, you wince and suck at it to make it feel better—in exactly the same spot that the frog deposited some of its lethal poison. In your weakened state, it is enough to kill you.

The end.

Poison Dart Frogs

- Poison dart frogs got their name because Amazonian people sometimes use the frogs' toxic secretions to poison the tips of their darts for hunting.
- All species of poison dart frog are small—from 0.3 to two inches (1 to 5 cm) in size—and all are very brightly colored, warning predators that they are poisonous. (A pity you didn't know that.)
- Three species of these frogs are dangerous to humans. The most poisonous is the golden poison dart frog, which is probably the most poisonous creature on Earth. It is only two inches (5 cm) long, but its skin contains enough poison to kill 10 adult humans.
- Many species of poison dart frogs are endangered.

You float swiftly down the river, carried by the current. You wonder why you didn't do this before. It's so much easier than making your way on land! There are no snakes to look out for, no thorny vines ripping your clothes, and no tree roots to trip over. Now that you are out of the forest and moving quickly, there are fewer biting insects, too. It feels great to be resting! You watch the trees and the muddy bank slide past you.

It's not long, though, before you begin to feel very hot. In the rainforest, you were protected from the sun. Now, with no trees to offer shade, the sun beats down relentlessly. Maybe you should make your way to the bank, stop, and find some way of making a sun shelter? On the other hand, it might be best just to keep going. You can put your waterproof coat over your head. Besides, who knows what other hazards you might find on the riverbank?

If you decide to stop the raft and make a shelter, go to page 93.

If you decide to keep going, go to page 82.

You find a long, sturdy stick and sharpen the end with your Swiss Army knife, trying to make as little noise as possible. You figure you must be downwind of the tapir because it doesn't seem concerned. It carries on rooting around on the forest floor. With your sharpened stick, you creep slowly and carefully toward the animal. A twig snaps and the tapir lifts its head, alarmed. You freeze. After a moment, the animal goes back to feeding. You creep forward again, your spear raised. You are just within range and you lunge forward for the attack . . . At the same moment, the tapir looks up and bolts, running straight at you in its panic and knocking your legs from under you! You fall forward, and the sharpened stick breaks underneath you, its tip sinking painfully into your leg.

The wound is deep and bleeding heavily. You are in extreme pain but force yourself to think–what should you do? You could make a bandage from your clothing, but your clothes are not sterile, and you might end up causing a fatal infection. Maybe you should try to find some clean water to wash the wound—but where?

If you decide to go in search of clean water, go to page 52.

If you decide to apply a bandage, go to page 60.

You are suffering from warm water immersion foot, which is much, much worse than a few blisters.

Walking gets more and more painful. Eventually, even though you want to keep going, you can't. You're forced to lie down. You're hot and exhausted and, by now, in extreme pain. You pass out. Unfortunately, not looking after your feet has spelled your doom . . .

The end.

Warm Water Immersion Foot

- Warm water immersion foot is very similar to tropical immersion foot, which was a common problem for American troops during the Vietnam War, when soldiers were constantly wading through paddy fields in army boots.
- It's also similar to trench foot, which people can get in wet, cold conditions. Its name comes from World War I, when soldiers had to stay for long periods of time in cold, muddy trenches dug into the earth.
- If any of these conditions aren't treated, the results can be very serious—sometimes resulting in amputation.
- Symptoms can include burning, numbness, swelling, and thickening and softening of the skin. The skin might also turn white or gray.
- One sufferer, Yossi Ghinsberg (see pages 120-121), said warm water immersion foot made his feet so painful that he dumped fire ants over his head so that their painful bites would take his mind off the agonizing pain in his feet!

Walking in the humid heat of the rainforest, you soon feel worse. You deeply regret eating that fruit. You stagger onward, getting weaker by the minute. You're in desperate need of water and gratefully drink the rainwater as it falls. But it's not enough to rehydrate you. You collapse and, eventually, you die.

The end.

It takes a bit of pushing with your stick to get over to the riverbank, making you feel even hotter and more exhausted. You're pouring with sweat, so you find some water to drink in a bamboo stem before you start to work.

You find a couple of large sticks to wedge in among the bamboo stems of your raft to form a simple tepee structure, then cover it with big, broad leaves. It looks messy, but it's not too heavy and it will provide you with shade, which is all that matters.

You push out into the river again, and soon nod off to sleep under your sunshade. You wake with a start! You've drifted over by the bank into shallow water, something is snorting just under the surface right in front of you! It looks like a small hippo. Your heart starts to race. Should you get out of the water, or steer your raft around the creature–whatever it is?

If you decide to move back into the river on your raft, go to page 112.

If you decide to get out of the water, go to page 100.

In fact this spider isn't a tarantula at all. It's a Brazilian wandering spider, and you've just woken it up! Alarmed, it scuttles toward your hand and bites you twice.

You cry out in pain and surprise. You are sure that tarantula bites aren't dangerous, but this bite feels very painful. Your hand soon starts to swell up. You notice you have started sweating even more than usual, too. You try to ignore it, but the pain gets worse, and your hand gets more and more swollen. Your activity is helping the spider's venom move around your body. Eventually, you collapse and die.

The end.

Brazilian Wandering Spider

- The Brazilian wandering spider was first discovered in Brazil but has turned up all over the world by traveling inside bunches of bananas. For that reason, they're also known as banana spiders.
- These spiders are nocturnal and use their venom to prey on insects, lizards, and mice. They hide in dark places during the day, then come out at night to hunt.
- Brazilian wandering spiders are sometimes mistaken for tarantulas because they're quite big—up to about five inches (12 cm) across—and hairy.
- The spiders often live near people, either in towns and villages or on plantations. They hide in dark places during the day, which makes them hard to see.
- They are probably the most venomous spiders in the world. They are also aggressive and can jump. Despite this, there aren't many human deaths from the spider's bite. But there is an antivenom available so, if a bite victim can get to hospital in time, they will probably be okay.

You watch as the monkeys sit in the branches high above you. They're eating, and a couple of them drop pieces of fruit and leaves before swinging off through the trees into the distance.

You go to examine the fruit the monkeys dropped. It looks a bit like avocado. Some pieces have bites taken out of them, but some are whole. Maybe you should eat some. After all, you and the monkeys are pretty closely related so, if it isn't poisonous to them, it shouldn't be poisonous to you, right? But only the whole pieces, you don't know what diseases the monkeys might be carrying.

If you decide to eat some of the monkeys' fruit, go to page 111.

If you decide not to, go to page 81.

Amazon Monkeys

- The monkeys that live in Central and South America have prehensile tails, which means they can wrap them around branches. This helps them swing from tree to tree. The monkeys in Africa and Asia don't have such a useful tail.

- There are hundreds of monkey species in the Amazon. The largest (and loudest) are howler monkeys.

- There are lots of different species of tamarin monkeys, most of which are about the size of a squirrel. The most recently discovered species is Mura's saddleback tamarin, discovered in 2009.

- Spider monkeys are thought to be some of the most intelligent monkeys. They grow to about 25 inches (65 cm) tall and have very long arms, legs, and tails—like a spider.

- The smallest monkeys in the world live in the Amazon. They are pygmy marmosets, which are only six inches (15 cm) long and weigh up to five ounces (140 g).

Panicked by the monkeys, you go crashing away from them in the opposite direction, not paying attention to where you're heading. Sharp thorns rip at your skin and clothes.

You come to a sudden and painful stop when you trip over a tree root, bashing your legs and falling to the ground. You stagger to your feet and look around you. The green rainforest canopy shows no signs of the monkeys. Your heart pounding, you decide to rest.

Go to page 106.

It isn't long before you spot another sign that people are around, and this one makes you even more hopeful! You see that there's a small hut on the riverbank, made from rusting corrugated iron. You start to push toward it. As you get closer, you see that there is a boat tied up to a rickety, wooden dock.

Go to page 113.

You jump from your raft onto the bank. Suddenly you panic, thinking that the creature might be able to get out of the water and chase you! You climb into the branches of a tree and watch. The animal is under the water, but you can still see the outline of its massive bulk. You wait awhile and watch, but the creature doesn't move at all. You're tempted to get back on your raft and move on, when a huge, bristly face emerges out of the water, takes a big gulp of air, and goes under again. You can see it a bit more clearly now and notice that it looks like an enormous seal! It certainly doesn't look aggressive.

As the animal submerges, you decide to risk it. You scramble back onto your raft and use your pole to push away as calmly as you can. Soon you're out of the shallow water and on your way, realizing that you've just been lucky enough to have a close encounter with an Amazonian manatee.

Go to page 107.

Amazonian Manatees

- Manatees are the Amazon's largest marine mammals. They are also known as sea cows because they're big, gentle, and they eat grass. They feed on underwater plants and algae.
- They never leave the water but do need to come up to breathe air. Manatees can stay underwater for up to 15 minutes!
- Amazonian manatees are the smallest of three species of manatee. The other two live in the Caribbean and Africa. But the manatees of the Amazon are still huge—up to nine feet (2.8 m) long and a whopping 1,100 pounds (500 kg) in weight!
- The only underwater vegetarian mammal, manatees have only molar teeth for chewing on plants. The teeth are replaced throughout their lives as the old ones wear down.
- Manatees were once hunted for their meat, oil, and bones. They're now quite rare.

You're feeling shaky after your encounter with the otters. Before long, you're hot and thirsty again as you continue down the river in the hazy sunshine. You start looking for a place to stop on the riverbank to find drinking water. As you search, you see something amazing! Barely visible under some low-growing trees, there's a small, battered-looking row boat!

Should you go over to the boat, which is moored in a tricky position, or stop a couple of hundred yards (meters) ahead, where there's a beach? After all, the boat does look old and could have been abandoned there because it won't stay afloat anymore.

If you decide to stop at the boat, go to page 113.

If you decide to carry on, go to page 99.

The tributary narrows and soon you have to use your pole to push since the current isn't strong enough to carry your raft along. It's tiring work. Should you stop for a rest, then turn around and go back the way you came? Or is it better to continue even though you're hot and tired?

If you decide to stop, go to page 110.

If you decide to carry on, go to page 114.

You tie up your raft on the riverbank, then swim toward the otters, which are calling noisily to one another. As you get closer, you realize they're much bigger than any otter you've ever seen before. In fact, they're huge—the size of an adult human! There are eight or nine of them in the group, and some of them are babies. Three of the adults are heading your way, swimming swiftly and strongly, making a low growling sound. You start to panic. Maybe they're worried about their young.

They're still some distance away. You turn and swim as fast as you can toward the raft, and clamber gratefully onto it. But the otters are still heading your way! They circle the raft several times as you push away from them as calmly as you can.

These are giant river otters, which can be aggressive and have been known to attack and kill dogs. Although they're not usually dangerous to humans, you were absolutely right to get away from them as fast as you could!

Go to page 102.

Giant River Otters

- Giant river otters are only found in South America in the Amazon, Orinoco, and La Plata river systems.
- They look very similar to North American otters, but with one major difference—they are up to six feet (1.8 m) long and weight up to 75 pounds (34 kg)!
- The otters feed mainly on fish, but also eat crabs and snakes and the occasional small caiman.
- They are also known as "river wolves," and sometimes hunt together as a pack.
- Giant otters sometimes attack dogs, but they're not usually a danger to people.
- These otters have a lot more to fear from people than we do from them. They've been hunted so much that they are now extremely rare.

You sit down on a log, feeling weak and sorry for yourself. After awhile, you feel a bit better. You spot a stand of bamboo not far away and decide to find some water in the stems to quench your thirst.

You're shaking the stems, listening for a sloshing sound that tells you there is water in the bamboo, when you spot a big, hairy spider only inches from your hand. You think it's probably a tarantula, and you know they aren't aggressive. Even if they do bite, their venom isn't dangerous.

If you decide to ignore the spider and carry on your search for water, go to page 94.

If you decide to go in search of some other bamboo, go to page 108.

You continue down the river on your raft, looking for signs of habitation as you go. You're sure that if you carry on downstream for long enough, you'll find people.

Before long, you are faced with a choice. Ahead of you, the river splits in two. Which route should you take?

If you choose the smaller of the two rivers, go to page 103.

If you choose the wider river, go to page 109.

You were right to be wary of the big, hairy spider in the bamboo. Tarantulas aren't aggressive and their bite isn't serious, but Brazilian wandering spiders are—and you've just met one. These kinds of spiders are aggressive and highly venomous (see page 95).

Luckily it's not long before you see some more bamboo, where you get some drinking water after checking carefully for spiders.

Go to page 81.

The river current carries you along. You gaze at the banks of the river, which are thick with trees. Soon you begin to see signs that make you hopeful! Trees are growing in regular lines, as though they've been planted. You spot a small boat moored to the bank! You can't see any people . . . but surely they can't be far away!

Go to page 114.

Tired, hot, and sweaty, you tie up your raft on the bank and sit down on a log for a rest. There are a few ants milling around. Suddenly you feel the most intense, blinding pain in your leg! It's agony! It happens again—and again! It's the ants!

You sink to the ground, writhing in pain, where more of the ants bite you. The ants' venom isn't enough to kill a person but, in your weakened, dehydrated state, with no one to help you, you pass out. Eventually, you die from dehydration.

The end.

Bullet Ants

- Bullet ants are a dark reddish brown in color and grow up to one inch (3 cm) long.
- Their sting is supposed to be the world's most painful insect sting—as painful as being shot by a bullet.
- The pain can last for 24 hours and can make people throw up and pass out.

Although it wasn't poisonous, the fruit has upset your stomach, and you vomit several times. You feel better afterward, but you know that it's important to replace the fluid you've just lost from vomiting. Should you stay and rest first or carry on in search of water?

If you decide to carry on, go to page 92.

If you decide to rest for a awhile then carry on, go to page 106.

As carefully as you can, you slide the stick into the water and push off. The creature has submerged, but you can still see its outline under the water's surface. Your heart is in your mouth as your raft glides past the large animal. You hardly dare to breathe.

In fact, the creature was a gentle manatee (see page 101), so you weren't in any danger. Soon, you're back in the river's swift current. In the distance ahead of you the river bends into a large loop, creating an wide area of slow-moving water. In the water, dark shapes dip and glide. You look more closely — they're otters! One of your favorite animals! You could stop and swim for a bit with the otters, which would cool you down and give you a wash at the same time.

If you decide to swim with the otters, go to page 104.

If you decide to carry on, go to page 107.

You tie up your raft and peer into the vegetation. You can't see anybody. You call out but there's no reply. People must be close by, though. You listen, but can only hear the strange whoops and cries of the rainforest animals.

You spot a narrow, well-worn trail leading along the riverbank. You don't want to stray too far from your raft, but you decide to take the trail and investigate.

Go to page 114.

You round a bend and, to your complete amazement, you see that there's a village on the riverbank! You rub your eyes, unable to believe what you're seeing. There are several huts, boats moored by the river, people cooking and talking, children running around, and chickens pecking at the ground!

It's not long before you're surrounded by helpful people offering food and water and tending to your wounds. You can't understand a word that anyone is saying, but you don't care! You're finally safe! The villagers contact an air ambulance, and it's not long before you're reunited with your family and friends. Your Amazon adventure is over at last.

The end.

The People of the Amazon Rainforest

More than 30 million people live in the Amazon, most of them in cities and towns. The biggest city is Manaus, with a population of 1.7 million. However, there are also people who live deep within the rainforest itself.

About a million native Amazonians live in the Amazon Rainforest in about 400 different tribes, each with its own language and culture. Some tribes have had contact with the outside world since Europeans first came to the Amazon around 500 years ago. Some still remain uncontacted in the vast rainforest. According to the Brazilian organization FUNAI (The National Indian Foundation (Brazil)), there are 67 uncontacted tribes in the Amazon. They hunt, fish, and farm in the same way their ancestors have done for thousands of years.

The first European settlers in South America enslaved or killed thousands of the people they found living there. The settlers also brought diseases such as smallpox, measles, and flu. The people of South America were not able to fight these new diseases, and many of them died.

Today Amerindian tribes are protected. FUNAI protects the lands where they live, and stops outsiders from going there uninvited. But logging and mining—some of it illegal—still continues—and it is destroying large areas of the rainforest.

Native Peoples of the Rainforest

Most Amazon tribespeople live in villages, where they grow crops, hunt, and fish. A few tribes are nomadic, traveling through the rainforest. These are just two of the hundreds of tribes of the Amazon:

- The **Ticuna** tribe was one of the first Amazonian tribes to meet the settlers from Europe in the sixteenth century. Today, despite their long history of contact with the outside world, they still have their own language and culture. They live near the borders of Brazil, Peru, and Colombia, in more than 70 different villages along a 620-mile (1,000 km) stretch of the Amazon.
- The **Yanomami** live in northern Brazil and southern Venezuela. They had no contact with the outside world until the twentieth century and live almost exactly as they did thousands of years ago. They're threatened by mining, logging, and cattle ranching, which destroy the rainforest. Workers also bring diseases that are common in the western world, but to which the Yanomami aren't immune. There are around 20,000 Yanomami, who live in 250 villages in the rainforest.

More Amazon Facts

As well as being the world's largest tropical rainforest, the Amazon is also the world's oldest. It is millions of years old and may have existed around the same time as the dinosaurs!

The Amazon Rainforest stretches across nine countries: Brazil, Bolivia, Peru, Colombia, Ecuador, Guyana, Suriname, Venezuela, and French Guiana.

There are different types of river water in the Amazon that are home to different types of marine life. Blackwater rivers flow through swamps and flooded forests, picking up acidic soil and sand on the way. This kind of river water is usually very pure. Whitewater rivers are a creamy color and contain lots of animal and plant life. Clearwater rivers don't contain many nutrients, so very few animals or plants can live in them. Where the blackwater Rio Negro (meaning black river) meets the whitewater of the upper Amazon, the two contrasting colors of water flow along together without mixing for about three and a half miles (6 km).

The Amazon Rainforest is home to millions of different plant and animal species, roughly including:

- 2.5 million insect species
- At least 40,000 plant species
- 3,000 fish species
- 1,300 bird species*
- More than 400 mammal species
- More than 400 amphibian species
- Nearly 400 reptile species

And new species are being discovered all the time. For example, in 2009, a new type of tamarin monkey was discovered.

*One in every five of the world's birds is native to the Amazon

Amazon Animal World Records

The amazing animals of the Amazon include:

- The world's largest eagle—the harpy eagle
- The world's smallest monkey—the pygmy marmoset
- The world's largest freshwater fish—the pirarucu
- The world's largest beetle—the titan beetle*
- The world's loudest monkey—the howler monkey

*The largest one measured was just over 6.5 inches (16.5 cm) —longer than a pygmy marmoset!

The Amazon is named after a race of fierce women warriors from Greek mythology—the Amazons. Spanish explorer, Francisco de Orellana reported seeing women warriors in the rainforest and named it after the mythical women.

There's a dry season and a rainy season in the Amazon. During the rainy season, from December to May, the difference in water level in some parts of the Amazon can be as much as an eight-story building.

Disappearing Amazon

As well as being an a beautiful place that teems with life, the Amazon Rainforest is essential to everyone and everything on the planet for many reasons:

- The world's rainforests are like its lungs, because they recycle carbon dioxide into oxygen. Without rainforests, the planet would die.
- A fifth of the world's fresh water comes from the Amazon basin.
- The Amazon's many different plant species have provided us with important medicines, including anti-cancer drugs. Only a small proportion of plants have been studied so far.

Despite its importance, an area the size of England is being destroyed in the Amazon every year. Trees are cut down for timber, then farms or cattle ranches take over the cleared land.

Real-life Rainforest Survival Stories

People have actually become lost in the Amazon, and some have lived to tell the tale. Here are two of their stories.

Juliane Koepcke was only 17 when the plane she was traveling in was struck by lightning and crashed in the rainforest in Peru. She woke up still strapped to her airplane seat, the sole survivor of the crash. All she was wearing was a mini dress and just one sandal. Her collar bone was broken, and she was covered in cuts and bruises. Regardless, she set off on foot to find help, using her single sandal to test the ground in front of her for snakes. She had no food, other than a few candies she found at the site of the plane crash. She walked through the Amazon Rainforest for 10 days, following streams and rivers downstream, before she found a deserted hut and a boat. By this time, a wound in her arm was crawling with maggots, and she used some gasoline she found in the hut to wash them out. The next day, some men turned up at the hut and took her by boat to the nearest town. She was taken by plane to a hospital and made a complete recovery. She lived in Germany, but later returned to Peru as a scientist, researching the bats of the rainforest.

Yossi Ghinsberg, from Israel, and three friends were searching for an uncontacted tribe in the remote Bolivian rainforest. They decided to split up—Yossi and his friend Kevin traveling by raft, the other two, Karl and Marcus, on foot. Yossi and Kevin lost one another when Yossi was swept over a waterfall on the raft.

Unable to find one another, Kevin eventually found his way to safety, then went back for Yossi with a rescue party. By the time they found him, Yossi had been alone in the rainforest for three weeks. He survived by eating fruit and birds' eggs. Once he had to scare off a jaguar, which he did by setting fire to some insect spray. He had a bad case of warm water immersion foot (see page 91), which he said was so painful that he dumped fire ants over his own head as a distraction from the pain. Sadly, the two friends who had set off on foot, Karl and Marcus, were never found.

Glossary

anticoagulant Something that stops blood from clotting

antivenom A product used to treat venomous bites and stings

balsa A tropical tree that has very light wood

caiman A crocodilian reptile

canopy The upper layer of trees in a forest

cholera A disease caused by bacteria in dirty water

contaminated Unclean

flash flood Sudden, quick flooding caused by very heavy rain

hallucinate Seeing things that do not really exist

meander Wander (winding and turning)

mildew A growth of mold

nomadic Not having one permanent home but moving from one place to another

paranoid Extremely anxious or afraid

parasites Creatures that live by attaching themselves to and feeding on other creatures

plantations Artificially grown forests or crop farms

predator A hunting animal

prehensile Able to grasp or hold

prey An animal that is hunted and eaten by another animal

receptors Parts of body cells that can receive signals

reticulated Covered with a netting pattern

ricin A poisonous toxin found in castor beans

secretion Storing then releasing a substance

stagnant Not flowing

tributaries Small rivers that flow into a larger, main river

vaccinated Protected (inoculated) against disease

venomous Capable of injecting venom

Learning More

Cherry, Lynne. *The Great Kapok Tree: A Tale of the Amazon Rain Forest.* HMH Books for Young Readers, 2000.

Dickinson, Rachel. *Tools of Navigation: A Kid's Guide to The History & Science of Finding Your Way.* Nomad Press, 2005.

Ghazoul, Jaboury, and Douglas Sheil. *Tropical Rainforest Ecology, Diversity, and Conservation.* Oxford University Press, 2010.

Kerr, P.B. The Eye of the Forest (Children of the Lamp). Orchard Books, 2009.

Khan, Hena. *Amazon* (The Worst-Case Scenario). Chronicle Books, 2012.

Simon, Seymour. *Tropical Rainforests.* HarperCollins, 2010.

Websites

A Kid's Wilderness Survival Primer (Equipped To Survive Foundation)
www.equipped.org/kidprimr.htm

How to Build a Survival Shelter
www.natureskills.com/survival/primitive-shelter/

List of great books about survival (Indianapolis Public Library)
www.imcpl.org/kids/blog/?page_id=12516

Survival Tips (I Shouldn't Be Alive—Animal Planet)
www.animalplanet.com/tv-shows/i-shouldnt-be-alive/videos/survival-tips-videos.htm

Spotlight: The Amazon (Kids Discover)
www.kidsdiscover.com/spotlight/the-amazon-for-kids/

Kids' Corner: games, virtual storybooks, activities, forest facts, plant and animal facts, and rainforests around the world (Rainforest Alliance)
www.rainforest-alliance.org/kids

Index